DEAD SPEED

CREATED BY KEITH AREM

PCB PRODUCTIONS PRESENTS

DEAD SPEED

www.dead-speed.com
www.pcbproductions.com

CREATED BY
KEITH AREM

ARTWORK
CHRISTOPHER SHY

WRITTEN BY
KEITH AREM
ADAM LAWSON

STARRING
YURI LOWENTHAL
MICHAEL IRONSIDE
NINA BERGMAN
STEPHANIE LYNN KATZ
TROY BAKER
ADAM LAWSON
JULIA AREM

POST-PRODUCTION
RYAN COOPER

SPECIAL THANKS
Valerie Arem, Katie Pruitt, Sean Davis, George Ruiz,
Ava Jamshidi, Lars Theriot, Nima Maleki, Peter Trinh,
Kristian Hedman, Brandon Humphreys, Matthew Brailey,
Lenny Brown, Danny Bilson, Laura Bailey, Travis Willingham,
Nolan North, Tara Platt, Liam O'Brien, Kari Wahlgren,
Matt Lemberger, Aaron Gallant, Matt Michelsen, Randy Stonitsch,
Ben Rekhi, Bruce Caspari, Alan Goldman, Paul Knell,
Dasha Shy, Pam Bowles, Arnold and Cynthia Arem

For Julia and Kyle

PCB PRODUCTIONS

- BUT YOUR DEAD WILL LIVE; THEIR BODIES WILL RISE.
YOU WHO DWELL IN THE DUST, WAKE UP AND SHOUT FOR JOY.-

-ISAIAH 26:19, NIV

HOME...

IT IS ALWAYS THE SAME.

THE SMELL OF FIRST RAIN.

THE SOUND OF THE WIND BLOWING THROUGH THE DRY WHEAT...

TIME SEEMS TO BE A FORGOTTEN VICE HERE.

WE'RE SAFE.

I NEED TO FIX THAT SQUEAKY STEP.

IT'S LEAH'S BIRTHDAY TOMORROW...

...CAN'T FORGET THE DRESS I PROMISED HER.

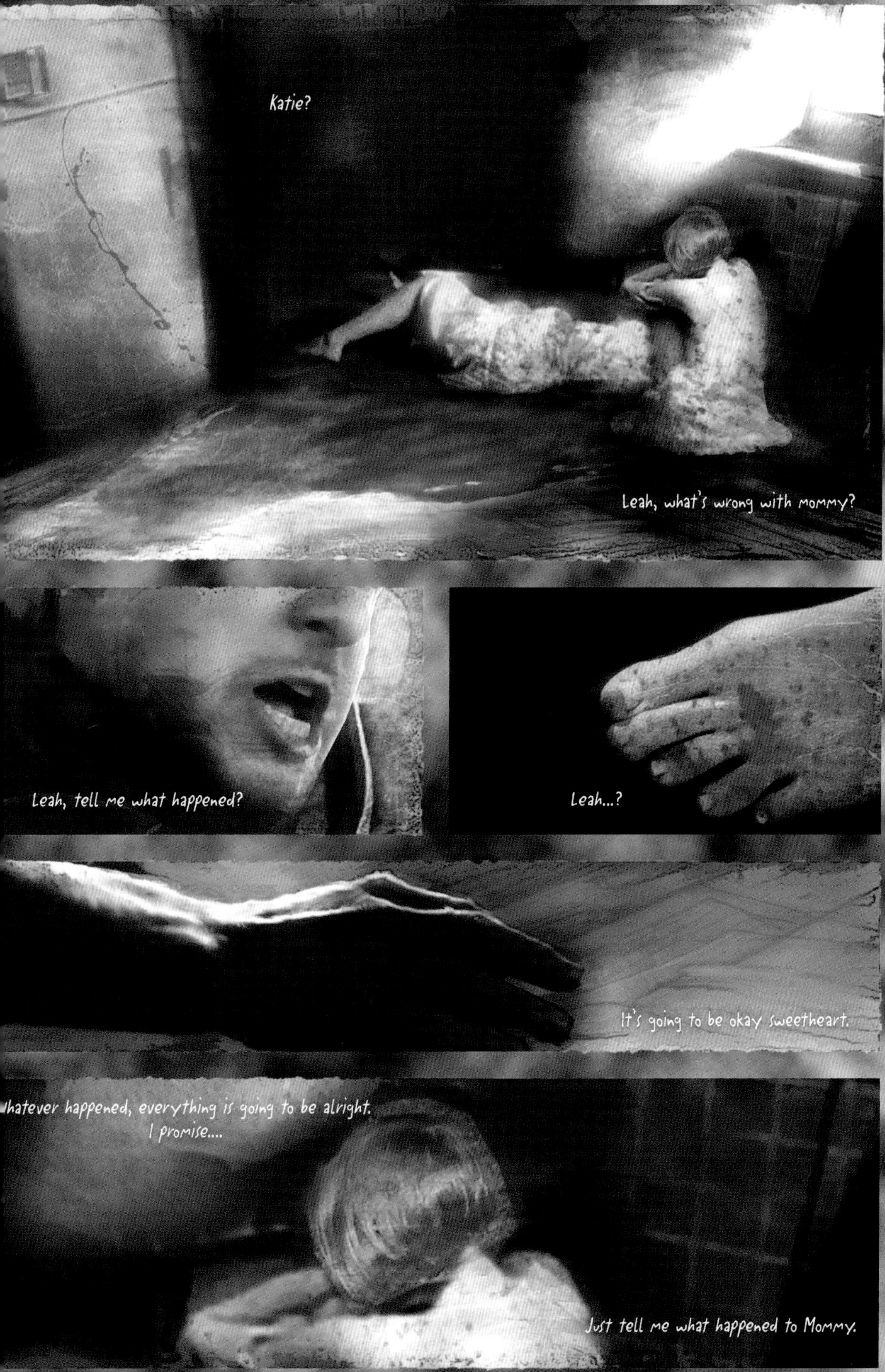
Katie?
Leah, what's wrong with mommy?
Leah, tell me what happened?
Leah...?
It's going to be okay sweetheart.
hatever happened, everything is going to be alright.
I promise....
Just tell me what happened to Mommy.

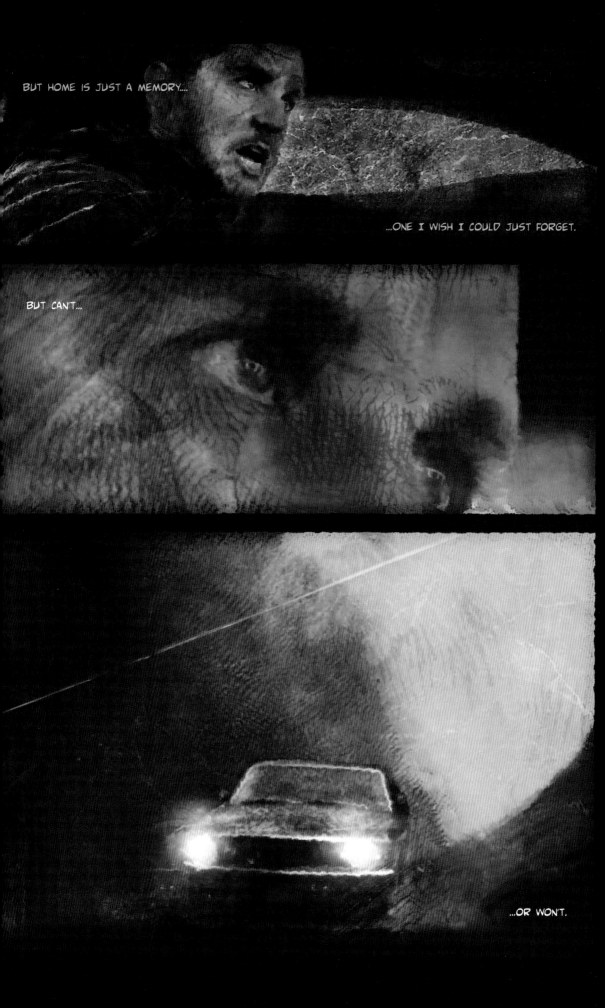

MY NEW HOME.
CHICAGO... OR WHAT'S LEFT OF IT.

NINETY-NINE PERCENT MORTALITY RATE FROM
THE AIRBORNE VIRUS CALLED "HOPE".
IRONIC, DON'T YOU THINK?

IT'S LIKE HUMAN KIND IS STARTING OVER,
AND THIS IS OUR GARDEN OF EDEN.

"HOPE" TAKES YOU DOWN A SINGLE ORGAN AT A TIME ONCE IT'S INFECTED MORE THAN TWO...YOU'RE DONE.

AND THAT IS EXACTLY THE KIND OF PERSON I'M LOOKING FOR... AN ORGAN "DONOR."

THIS IS THE FARTHEST I'VE EVER BEEN FROM THE COMPOUND.

WHO KNOWS WHAT'S SURVIVED OUT HERE...

BEEP ... BEEP ....

FUE

THAT'S A PROBLEM...

FUCKING SEARCHER KEEPS POINTING TOWARDS SOMEONE....BUT I AIN'T SEEING IT...

...GOT HER.

YOU GOTTA LOVE THE FLORA AROUND HERE.

THEY KEEP US RIPPERS ON A SHORT LEASH... JUST ENOUGH GAS FOR EIGHTY MILES.

ROSSMORE: CHICAGO'S MAXIMUM SECURITY PRISON. WE KNOW IT AS THE COMPOUND.

ALL THOSE CONCRETE WALLS AND BARBED WIRE 'FENCES ACTUALLY SAVED US. WHAT KEPT US BAD GUYS IN, HELPED KEEP THE FLESH EATERS OUT.

WHEN RHYS AND THE MILITARY ASSHOLES CAME IN, THEY GAVE US A CHOICE: RIP ORGANS OR TAKE OUR CHANCES OUTSIDE THE WALL. HELL OF A WAY TO EARN OUR FREEDOM.

LIKE I SAID, I'M A COWARD.

THEY SAY WE'RE THE LAST STAND. THE LAST REFUGE. BUT WHAT THE FUCK DO "THEY" KNOW ANYWAY.

ODOMETER SAYS EIGHTY-TWO RIGHT NOW...

...IT'D SUCK TO PUSH THIS PIECE OF SHIT THE LAST FOUR HUNDRED YARDS.

DOC SAYS ORGANS GO BAD IN TWENTY MINUTES.
REALLY DOESN'T HELP WITH THE PRESSURE OF HAVING
TO GUT INNOCENT PEOPLE WHILE WE KILL ZOMBIES...
...FOR ALL WE KNOW THEY COULD'VE BEEN A COUSIN
WE FORGOT FROM THE LAST FAMILY REUNION.

...SEVEN MINUTES AND COUNTING.

Gray, What'd you get?

Heart and liver.

That's all? No lungs?

Party got crashed by uninvited guests.

Seventy five for both.

Bullshit. Two bills at least. I lost my windshield on the run.

A bit steep. I'll give you half.

Gimme the heart back.

This is someone's life we're talking about.

It's mine too, asshole.

Fine, but don't forget we're in this together,
Ripper. Someday you may need one of these.

That happens...you let me die.

I'm clean.

We still need to check.

And what happens if I'm not? You kill me?

No.

We've saved over two hundred people
in the last nine months. We're making a difference.

Course not. You'll just harvest me.
I'm an ex-con. Fuck him, right?

Darren, It's not like that.

And you weren't before?

No. I was just a medic, sitting
on the sidelines waiting to matter.

You certainly got that now –

Back off. I know they treat you guys
like shit, but I'm on your side.
And if you really don't care,
why the midnight runs?

They're suicide missions. You've ripped more
organs than any three runners...

...Don't tell me it's for the money
because I know what they pay you.

Thanks for the meds. Can I go now?

Heart is stable, Dr. Rhys. Ready for the transplant.

Prepare her for plasma extraction.

But, she's lost a lot of blood, sir.

Noted...
Connect the plasma tube.

Dr. Rhys...The surgery isn't complete.
Why an extraction now? We should wait
until she's clear or she won't make it.

Do not question me, Richards. Plasma tube, now.

Yes, sir.

You have good intentions, but you lack the vision.
In time you will understand.

Who was the harvester on this organ?

Darren Gray, sir.
He made an unsanctioned
run near the edge of the zone.
The Rippers are running out of donors
close to the compound.

He's quite prolific.

Yes, he is sir.

Excuse me, Dr. Rhys. I was finishing with a Ripper vaccination.
You wanted to see me?

Dr. Evans -

What can you tell me about Darren Gray?

SIX RIPPERS AND ONLY ONE DONOR. PICKINGS ARE GETTING SLIM.

THIS ISN'T OVER...

HE'S NOT GOING AFTER THE DONOR.

CRASH

GGRRRRHHHH!!!!

Yeah, I know.
I spoiled your lunch

BANG!!!!

Aahhh!

I can't feel my legs...

Yep.

I'm bleeding.

So, it hurts.
Now get your ass up.

That too.

I LOST THE DONOR RUN, AND JAKE WILL STILL TRY
TO SLIT MY THROAT THE FIRST CHANCE HE GETS.

BEING THE GOOD GUY SUCKS.

PLACE STILL LOOKS LIKE A PRISON.

...I'm... not gonna.. make it...

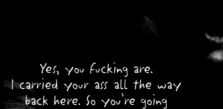

Yes, you fucking are.
I carried your ass all the way
back here. So you're going
to survive goddamnit.

I got a Ripper in critical. I need help!

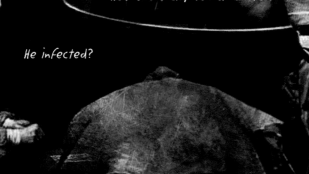

Vitals stabilizing.
He's one lucky son of a bitch.

He infected?

Won't know for 48 hours.
We'll move him to ISO so
we can keep an eye on him.

If he had come in 5 minutes later,
he wouldn't have made it.

I was hoping he wouldn't.

Didn't you bring him in?

Yeah.

I wasn't held enough as a baby.

How did a man like you end up in maximum
security... You're not like the others.

I would like to offer
you a special assignment, Gray.

Find someone else...I'm busy.

I think you misunderstand what I'm offering.
I'm providing a way out of being a harvester
and into becoming a part of my elite team.

I need someone with your skills and I believe I can
trust you. And that makes you special. Even Dr.
Evans agrees with me on that.

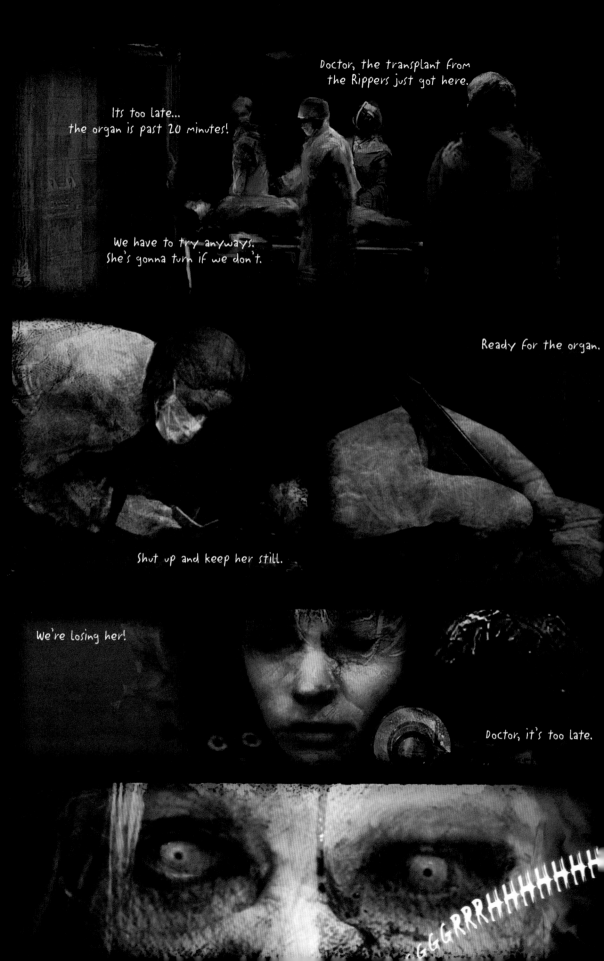

URGHH!!!
HELP!!!!
RIPP
Please God, no. PLEASE!
Hey!
GGGRRRHHH...
GGGRRRHHH!!!

freeze! Drop the goddamn weapon!

You shot a woman in cold blood.

I just saved your life, asshole.

Are you fucking blind? She turned!

It's clear you're a threat to life at Rossmore. Murder is punishable by death. Take him away.

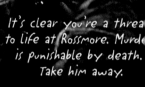

Dr. Rhys, there's someone on the short wave for you.

Put it on intercom. Clear the room.

IF IT'S NOT HERE IN TWENTY-FOUR HOURS THIS WHOLE FUCKING FACILITY IS GONNA COLLAPSE.

WHAT THE FUCK'S GOING ON, RHYS? WE'RE ALMOST OUT! THEY'RE DRAINING HER!

That's not an option. You'll have the shipment.

Maintain your post, Captain. I said it's on it's way.

I need you to make a run.

I can stop your execution.

I was looking forward to it.

But first, I'm going to have them kill Kristin.

My answer is still go fuck yourself.

You just had to go there, didn't you?

I don't think I need to impress upon you the importance of secrecy.

But you're going to anyways.

I believe this might be the chance you've been waiting for.

What is this?

TAK40 assault vehicle. Bullet proof. Twenty-six hundred horse power. On a full tank it can travel four hundred and eighty miles.

This looks like Searcher technology. Where did you get it?

Welcome to a whole new world Mr. Gray.

This a stick? –

I am sure you'll
get the hang of it.
I need you to make a
delivery outside
of the zone.

What's on the other side?
I thought we were the last
survivors on earth.

We are.

The trunk is combination sealed and cannot
be opened. The destination is pre-programmed
into the NAV system key.

When you arrive, there will be a docking station.
Connect the vehicle and the machines will do the rest.

What's inside the
trunk, Rhys?

Despite what you believe, Darren,
I am not a bad man.

Be careful. Once you
leave the zone, things
will change.

Whatever you say.

They already have

OH SHIT...

...SO THIS IS THE PART WHERE I DIE.

SHE'S MAYBE SIXTEEN...

...LEAH WOULD HAVE BEEN FOURTEEN.

PLASMA EXTRACTION

WHAT ARE THEY DOING TO YOU?

I'm getting you out of here.

You OK?

mmmhhh...

Yeah, not really the time
for conversation. I get it.

IF WE MAKE IT TO THE OTHER SIDE OF THE WALL, THE SEARCHERS WON'T SEE US.

BUT THE WALKERS WILL... BRILLIANT RESCUE PLAN, ASSHOLE.

YEAH...
SHOULD HAVE LEFT HER.

GGGGRRRRHHHH...

REMEMBER, YOU'RE NOT A FUCKING HERO.

LIKE I GOT OPTIONS.

BOOM BOOM

It's gonna get loud for a minute, Miss.
Sorry, should have said something.

Hold onto my hand.

DAMN, I'M TURNING... HAPPENING FAST.
I CAN ALREADY FEEL THE INFECTION SETTING IN...

GGGGGGGGGRRRRRRHHHHHH!!!!

Gotta find someplace to hide her.

SLAMM!!!

Just go!

THEY DIDN'T SHOOT ME, WHICH MEANS THEY WANT TO TALK...

Aren't you guys supposed to be helping us?

...WHICH MEANS I'M REALLY FUCKED.

TALKS OVER.

SHINK!

SKREEEEEE!!!!!!

MY GUTS FEEL LIKE SOMEONE TOOK A BLENDER TO THEM, MY VISION IS BLURRING AND I'M BEING CHASED BY THE ONLY GUYS WALKERS ARE SCARED OF...

YOU COULD SAY I'M AT A LOW POINT IN MY LIFE.

Hey kid, if you can hear me, we're leaving!

THE VIRUS DECIDED TO GO
FOR MY LUNGS FIRST.

BUT I GOT BIGGER PROBLEMS.

FEELS LIKE I'M BREATHING
STEAM THROUGH A PLASTIC BAG.

NRRRGGGGHHH...

HOME.

AT LAST.

Leah...Daddy's home. You ready to go riding today? I missed you so much.

Where's Mommy? Leah, Is everything OK?

No. God. Please. No.

BLAM!

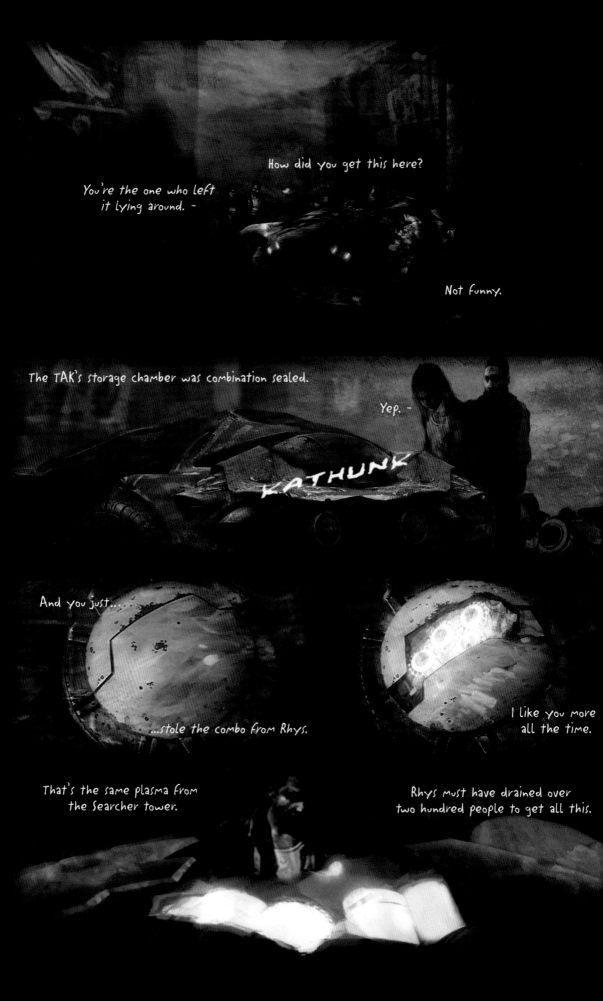

Ahhhhhhh!

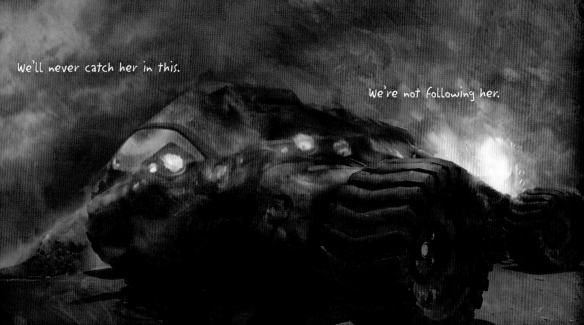

Their right behind us!

You know how to handle an assault cannon?

I'm a solider.

Then get your ass up there.

She's not your daughter, Darren.

I KNOW.

SHH!!!

You can relax...
They're not following us anymore.

What was your family like?

They're dead. Let's leave it at that.

All we have is what's here
and now, you know?

All I have is the memory of losing
the people I loved.

Good to know we're in this together...
Enjoy feeling sorry for yourself.
I'm gonna take a look around.

What do you have?

Empty plasma containers,
cabinet's full of them.

From the injection dates...
...they've been empty a long time.

Why would Searchers be carrying plasma vials?

Maybe it's what they eat....
...Maybe that's why Rhys sent you.

How far to go?

30 miles.

Something huge on the NAV ahead...

Looks like a military complex or some kind of underground installation.

How are we on weapons?

I got four loaded shells and then I'm out.

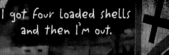

Perfect.

This is where Rhys programmed the TAK to deliver the plasma?

DO NOT
ENTER

⚠DANGER

I was hoping for the Emerald City.

Oh my god, what the hell are those?

Looks like this batch didn't make it...
maybe they ran out of food....

...Too many mouths to feed.

But what were they doing to them?

I don't know. It has the same
plasma matrix as the green tower...

...These tubes lead into that
chamber at the end of the hallway.

Searchers. Some sort of incubation chamber...
I think they were breeding them here.

Look at the skeletons...

...These things started out human.

Maybe they were working on
a feeding system.

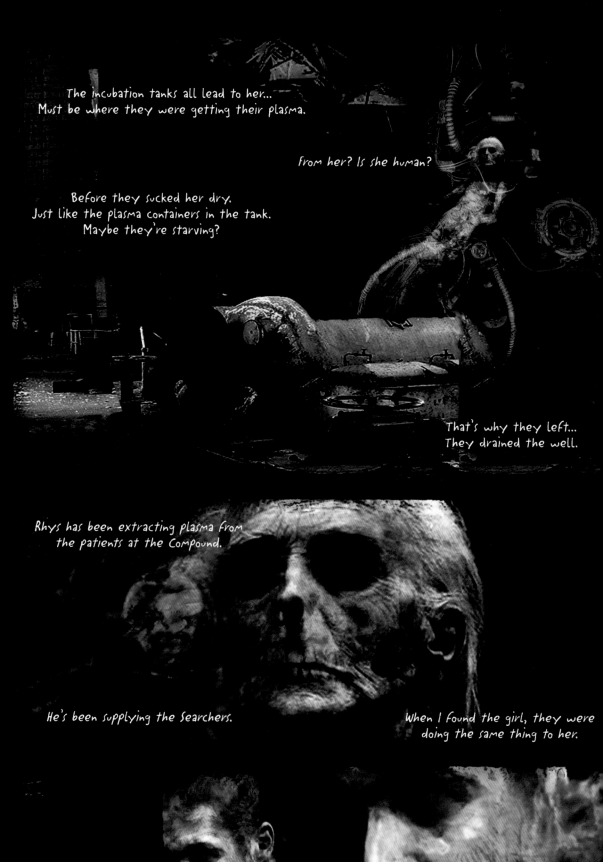

The incubation tanks all lead to her...
Must be where they were getting their plasma.

From her? Is she human?

Before they sucked her dry.
Just like the plasma containers in the tank.
Maybe they're starving?

That's why they left...
They drained the well.

Rhys has been extracting plasma from
the patients at the Compound.

He's been supplying the Searchers.

When I found the girl, they were
doing the same thing to her.

They're going to drain her
like they did this woman.

We have to go.

Walkers got into the base.

I'm thinking we leave.

Yeah.

Go - Now!
Get your ass moving

THREE SHELLS LEFT AND ABOUT EIGHT HUNDRED WALKERS TO GO...

...PERFECT.

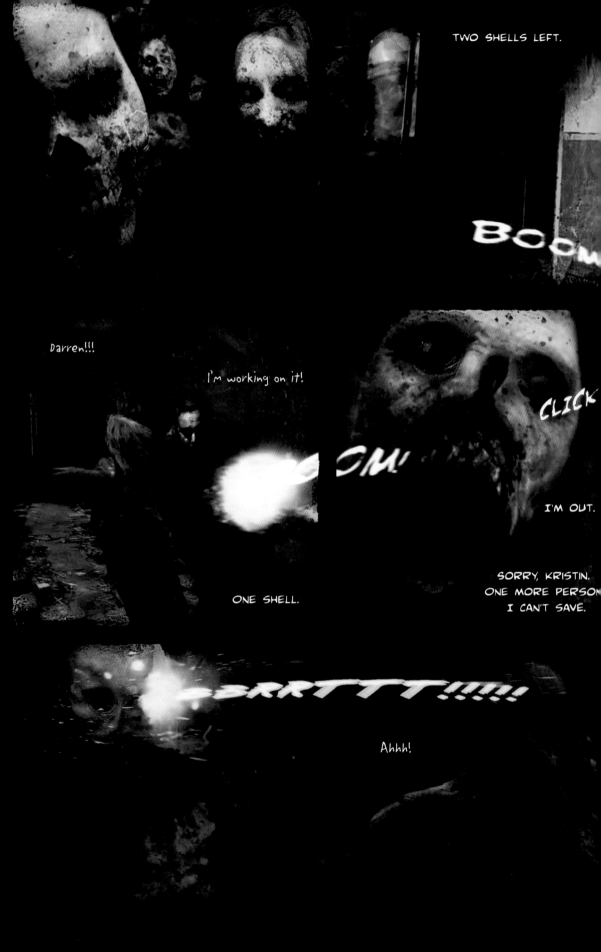

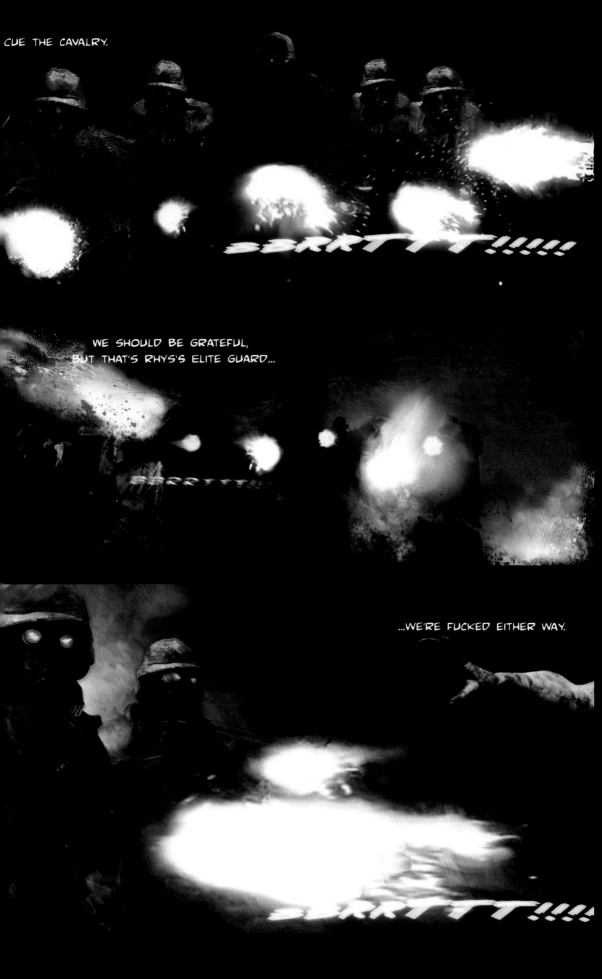

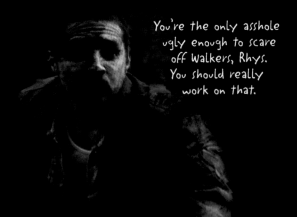

You're the only asshole
ugly enough to scare
off Walkers, Rhys.
You should really
work on that.

There are greater concerns
than your contempt for me. Where's Eve?

Who's Eve?

My daughter. The girl you stole.

Your daughter? Her blood can cure the Hope virus.

I know. Where is she?

Searchers took her.

You selfish idiot. All you had to do was deliver
a single cargo load. Now Rossmore is lost and
we are at war with the Searchers.

At war?
What are you talking about?

You used us like cattle
to keep those fucking
things alive?

Those things kept US alive.
But, you had to be the
hero didn't you? Well, your
blind act of "heroism" has
condemned all of us.

We had a truce. We supplied
the Searchers with plasma,
and they kept the Walkers out.

What happened to the Compound?

They're dead. When you took Eve...
the Searchers attacked us without warning...

...The Walkers cleaned up the rest.

My men and I barely managed to escape.

And you conveniently made your way here.

This was the last of our research facilities.
Hope tried to keep them alive.

Hope? She was your wife?
She was connected to the plasma extractors.
You were never working on a cure for the Hope virus.

I'm the one who created it.

You fucking bastard.

Don't pretend to have a false sense of morality.

Don't you remember the waste, the crime,
the disease, the traffic, the overpopulation.
It was a matter of time before
the planet wiped itself clean.

We were all dying before Hope ever existed.

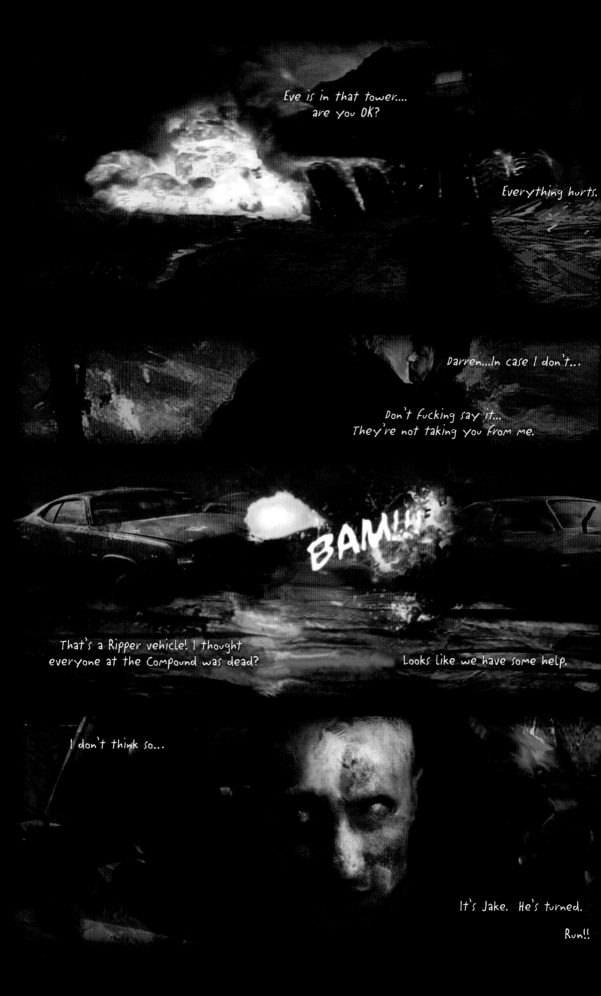

VVVRRROOOOOOOOMMMMMM!!!!!!!

The plasma feeds run down this corridor.

Eve must be down there.

DINNER IS SERVED BOYS AND GIRLS.

GGRRHHHH

FOR A MOMENT I FEEL ALIVE. LIKE A FATHER AGAIN.

A FATHER WHO SEES HIS CHILD IN DANGER.
A FATHER WHO NOW HAS SOMETHING TO LOSE.

Eve! My god...
What have they done to her?

We have to get her out of there.

How? We could kill her.

She's going to die if we don't get her out.

That's not an option.

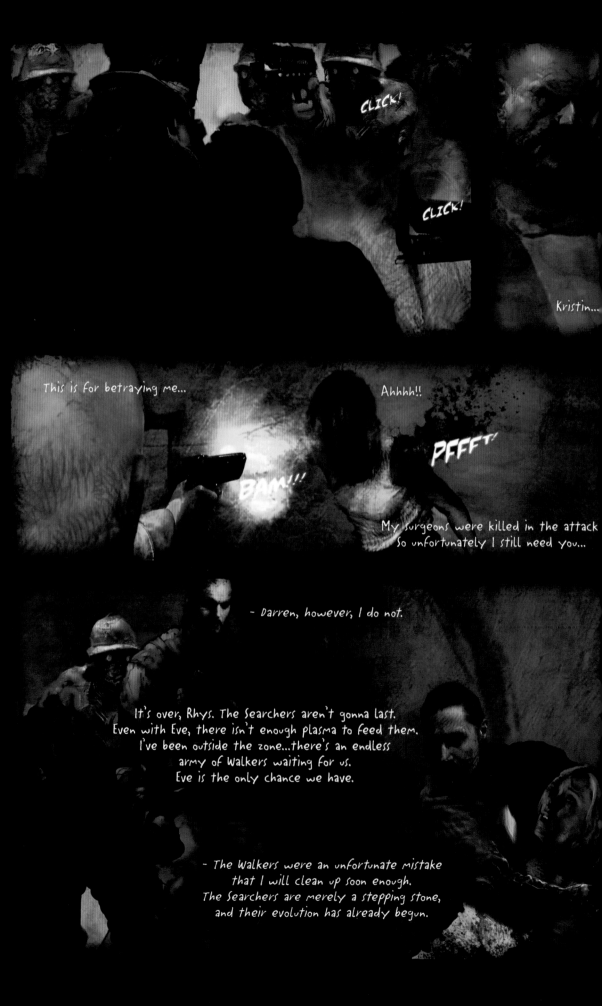

What evolution? The Walkers are
tearing them apart.

I created the Searchers to stop mankind
from destroying themselves... but their majesty was
flawed by their dependence on plasma.

"Hope" was an attempt to fix that and
it lightened the path to The Tree of Life.
We found the key to immortality...

Immortality?
"Hope" wiped out 7 billion people, Rhys. –

A bonus. Death solves all problems.
The Walkers were an unforseen bi-product
of "Hope," but couldn't be controlled.
I now know how to correct that error.

Then why do you need Eve? –

She will keep the Searchers alive
long enough for me to
finish what I have begun...

...Which you will
not be around to witness.

Darren! No!!!
BLAM!
GHHRK!
BLAM!
Shoot them! Dammit, kill them!
BLAM! BLAM!
Eve!
What have you done?
AND THE CREATOR...
...IS NOW...
AAHHHHH!!
...CONSUMED BY HIS CREATON.

Darren! Her heart stopped!

ARE WE OUT OF MIRACLES?

MANKIND'S LIFE CLOCK
DOWN TO IT'S FINAL SECONDS.

Hang on Eve...We're not going
to let you die..

SHE'S ALL WE HAVE TO REBUILD HUMANITY,
BUT ALL I CARE ABOUT IS SAVING MY NEW DAUGHTER.

Please hurry!

Please, hold on.

Hold on Eve...

EVERYTHING BECOMES A BLUR...

...AND THEN GOES DARK.

KEITH AREM

Dead Speed was created by writer, producer, and creative director Keith Arem.
President of Los Angeles based PCB Productions, Arem is a leading
creator and digital post-production supervisor for the interactive community.
He served as Director of Audio for Virgin Interactive Entertainment
and Director of Audio for Electronic Arts Pacific.

Arem has produced and recorded over 500 commercial releases in the film,
music, and interactive industries, including: Call of Duty Modern Warfare series,
Ghost Recon series, Ultimate Spiderman, Spiderman The Movie, X-Men series,
Lord of the Rings, Tony Hawk Pro Skater series, Everquest 2, Splinter Cell 3,
Prince of Persia series, Spriggan, Disney's Emperor's New Groove, Metal Arms,
.Hack//Sign, X-Files On-line, Ridge Racer, and Contagion's Infectant.
Arem's clients include: Sony, Activision, Microsoft, UbiSoft, Universal, Disney,
Nintendo, Boeing, Namco, Capitol, Ubisoft, Electronic Arts, and Fox.

Arem's recent graphic novels include Ascend, Infex, and Frost Road.

CHRISTOPHER SHY

Artist Christopher Shy is an illustrator, painter, and writer, who has worked in
comics, games, and film since 1993. President of Studio Ronin, Shy's recent
work includes X-Men, Black Panther (Marvel Comics), Resistance (DC Comics),
and products for White Wolf, Arbor Sports, and Sims Snowboards.

Shy has completed two graphic novels for Studio Ronin and
is the creator of Man to Leaves, Seven Leaves, Syndicate Has No Face,
Hateful Youth, AunJnu, and Apokolpse Ant. Shy was voted Artist of the Year at
Origins, and spot lighted as Artist of the Year for White Wolf Games.
In 2003, Shy was chosen for the prestigious cover of Wisconsin
Review by the University of Wisconsin. Shy's clients include: Microsoft,
Marvel Comics, DC Comics, LucasArts, White Wolf Productions,
Russell Productions, UbiSoft, Red Storm, and many others.